Eros & Psyche: a myth of love lost and won

by Lisa Peers

Printed in the United States of America

First printing: 2016

ISBN-13: 978-1530051670
ISBN-10: 1530051673

For my love

.

୫୨୯୫

I always have been. Always, I will be.

I existed as pure energy alongside the undefiled plains of Gaia, the dark prison of Tartarus and the extreme absence of Chaos. They were apart, singular, without connection, without companionship or purpose. The ache of separateness was agony.

I caressed Gaia's broad body and retreated. Lonely without my touch she created Ouranos as a lover to spread over her, gaze starry-eyed at her beauty and engender children through sensual pleasure. She became Mother Earth because of me.

Yet Ouranos' unrelenting appetites became Gaia's affliction. He forced himself on her day and night. He buried their monstrous progeny deep within her, trapping them in her caverns. His jealousy and shame over his

5

children became a burden Gaia could not endure. She convinced her son Kronos to castrate his father and free her from his licentious bondage. Kronos' sickle fell and Ouranos' screamed, his blood and semen cast into the vast ocean. Out of the carnage the Erinyes took wing, borne of violence and spite to ruin the lives of the sinful.

But another wave brought forth a much different creature. Aphrodite rose from the ocean, flowers drifting in her wake, her sea-foam eyes cherishing beauty in all things and happiness in all forms.

I was attracted to her, not as a man to a woman but as an orphan child to a safe haven. I needed guidance and hope. Above all else I was lonely.

Aphrodite opened her arms and gathered me to her, calling me Son. She shaped me into a cherub, bidding me start afresh as a winged child to grow and learn of the treasured delights of beauty and pleasure. She taught me to channel my power through a slender bow and arrow. She would guide and direct me, and I would be more judicious in bestowing my awesome gifts.

I am now my mother's servant. No longer an impish boy, I have a man's height and strength with the wings of a swan rooted in my back. I disguise myself to fly unseen and silent to mingle among the mortals and gods alike, my arrow spurring them to act on their impulses, to kiss and stroke and procreate, to revere physical passion and emotional bliss, to connect.

I am Longing and Yearning. I am Hope and Wish and Want. I am Eternal Desire.

I always have been. Always, I will be.

I am Eros.

I am Psyche.

I am a daughter, so I must follow my father's path for me. I am the daughter of a king, so I must marry and marry well. I am fortunate to be deemed beautiful, and so I must enjoy the attention of potential husbands. It is expected.

So why am I so relieved that my suitors have disappeared?

They had been thick at the door for weeks, loitering at the market, passing the host of a banquet or the bride and bridegroom at a wedding to give me their attentions instead. They were a varied lot with handsome and wealthy men among them, all made foolish by an allure I never cultivated nor wished for. I was polite to the extreme, greeting them kindly then making my apologies as I shut the gate or stole through a side door before locking it behind me.

My father required me to speak to a few men he deemed credible, so of course I complied. Once their stores of flattery were exhausted, though, their true selves came to the fore. Some were courting my father's money: that became plain very quickly. Others wished a position in my father's kingdom. I could have been a basket of figs or a sack of grain to barter at the market for how they spoke of me.

There were some, though, who earned my sympathy if not

my heart. What they sought was a simple girl who could nurture their dreams until she became a woman who would not laugh at their mistakes. I wished them well and sent them away.

None appealed to me. There was no kindling of interest on my side, no sparking of minds. I was holding on to hope that, despite the duty, there could be mutual attraction, excitement of some kind. Joy. Desire.

That is what the gods enjoy. I learned this from my father's stories of their conquests. Each is overcome with an overwhelming urge to be with one that the Fates have destined for him. Of course the gods are far more illicit than the women they pursue; thus is the way of the mortal world as well. Yet goddesses, too, have their lovers, prodded by Eros' arrow.

I have heard tell of sex. Not from my sisters; they were righteous virgins until their wedding nights then later pursed their lips when I would ask of the mechanics of pregnancy and birth. The household servants were much better at putting words to the mysteries of physical love, although often it was easier for them to explain by showing me pigs during the spring rut than describe the incandescent attraction that I hear surrounds fortunate lovers.

Not that I will know these secrets myself any time soon, for one day the suitors were clamoring and the next they were gone. Then another day of solitude, then a week, then a month. Now my father is alarmed. His aim is to ensure I am well married and cared for when he is gone. He fears I will wither without male company.

Today we will go to the Oracle at Delphi. The Oracle's prophecy is often cryptic and rarely reassuring. To my mind it is better to let the Fates reveal what will happen day by day rather than living in fear of when a dread prediction will come true. This is not my father's way, though, and my opinion does not sway him.

The journey starts before noon, and I need time to collect my thoughts. I walk to the cliff near my father's house, where the waves pummel the boulders and birds skitter across the sky. The sun's warmth is soothing as I sit on top of a smooth rock high above the rest. I close my eyes and tilt my head back so the breezes caress my face.

Despite my misgivings, I am excited by our trip. Good or ill, I will discover my destiny, which means I will have a future that is my own.

###

I serve my mother; that is my place in the universe. I receive no prayers—that is her responsibility—and I am a tool at her disposal to answer those that come to her. If she deems a request worthy I am sent with the arrows steeped in passion to begin a romance that may last a human's lifetime.

For millennia I never stayed to see the result of my arrow finding its mark. I had others to set in my sights; I had no need to see if the love match were good or ill for that was my mother's purview. There were too many beings, celestial and terrestrial, who required my services.

After being part of my mother's retinue for so long,

though, I became curious. I asked her what happened after I winged away, and she was happy to show me. We sat at the edges of humanity, observing the lives of those I had brought together. Some matches were spectacularly bad: the initial attraction dried up like grass in a drought, or one member of the pair could not stay loyal, or became violent or shrewish or simply uninterested.

Yet there were far more couples who used love as a touchstone for life itself. Whatever calamities occurred, however they were buffeted by loss and pain, their partnership kept them certain that all was not for naught. They husbanded their attraction to each other and tended the flame of desire within their hearts throughout their lives. It could flare into passion or burn low and warm as romance or kindness. It never went out. It sparked poems and good deeds. It was physical in a thousand different ways. That connection could even supersede death: after Hades claimed each of them, my mother told me, they'd find each other in the shady dim of the underworld and stay together, hand in hand, unwilling to allow their beloved to spend a moment bereft of company. It was unspeakably lovely.

Each story added resolve to my longing for a companion, a lover, a wife. Someone whose body would fit well within my embrace; someone whose pleasure would be my own. Someone who would bear us a child to cherish together; someone who would see the universe as I did and could be at my side to talk and laugh and touch. I longed for this more than I could express. With each launch of my arrow for others, I sought one who could join me on my journey. Despite my mother's company and that of the many residents of Olympus, I would go home alone. Loneliness would gnaw at my heart many nights, much as it did when I was without form.

I have not tasted of the joy and pleasure I grant to gods and humans. I desire it for myself. But until that moment comes, I serve my mother as she dictates.

For those who worship her well, Mother is benevolent and tender. She bestows companionship to the friendless. She provides family and children to those who are alone. She watches over some humans from birth then sheds tears when they die. To her devotees she is kindness itself.

Yet to those who do not show her proper favor, she is petty and cruel. Small slights buzz around her head like flies circling ripe fruit, fouling it when they land. Thus when her temples are more empty than full or her pyre is not alight with ample offerings, she becomes relentlessly nasty, bent on making a poor wretch suffer—even if the crime is simply the sin of being as beautiful as she is.

This is the cause of my malicious errand for the morning.

A human girl named Psyche, reported to be of good breeding and great beauty, recently became of marriageable age and drew the attention of many a man. They bid to worship her rather than the Goddess of Love, stoking my mother's wrath. Rather than punish the suitors she aims to punish the girl.

First she cast a spell over the girl's dwelling to send suitors away in droves. I am to deliver the second portion of punishment. Mother bids me drive an arrow into the girl's heart just in time for her to spy a boar or a crab or a lizard scuttling across the sand—whatever horrid creature that would humiliate her most for falling in love with it.

I find her seated on a cliff, vulnerable and alone. I scan around for a dreadful candidate for her infatuation and spy a spider picking a leggy path through the rocks. Pleased with my choice I secretly float in front of her to set my arrow at the ready, knowing my mother would want the arachnid to bite the girl on the toe for good measure.

Eyes closed, her head is tilted back in the sunshine, her lips apart as if waiting for a kiss from Helios himself. Her hair is loose, streaming behind her like a skein of fine linen. I fly closer. Her face fascinates me. It is so much softer than my mother's, less aloof and more inviting.

My shadow falls over her and with its sudden chill her eyes fly open as if startled from a dream. Her dark eyes search the air and without knowing it, she casts her gaze on me. She is exquisite: her eyes, her face, her body are all bathed in grace and dignity. I could look at her forever and be happy.

Pain shatters my reverie: my arrow has scratched my palm. I cry out as overwhelming pleasure rolls over me like a thunderstorm. Swooning, I drop from the sky, nearly plunging into the sea before I right myself, my breath quick and my head pounding. Her beauty makes all I have done in the name of love seem pitiful and pointless.

The girl is on her feet, dashing away from the rock and my presence to answer her father's call. I fly after her, not wishing to lose the sight of her for a moment. She shuts the door before I can lay a hand to stop her. I fly around the palace but find no door ajar, no window cracked through which I can enter. I am bereft.

I hear an elder male voice bidding her to take her shawl and cover her head, for the Oracle will not stand for impudence. I gather they wish the priestess' vision to define her destiny.

I am shot with the poison of love. I am that destiny. So I hatch a plan.

I speed to Delphi and touch down in front of the Oracle's seat. She is haughty and impenetrable, a bastion of virtue and truth.

"Oh beautiful prophetess, I seek your assistance."

"Eros, you cannot sway me," she says with an indulgent air. "My chastity in the service of Apollo makes me uninterested in anything you have to offer."

"I disagree," I say, my charm honey-sweet. "I have the power to inspire not just romantic love but creation as well."

"Why would this interest me?"

"Surely you would appreciate more mortals knowing of your pure purpose, your command of what is true and right. Certainly a poem or song heralding your name would be pleasing to you."

The Oracle may be chaste but she is still a woman who craves flattery. "You can guarantee this?"

"Most certainly."

The proud priestess' resolve falters. "What is you would wish, Eros? You know I cannot lie on your behalf."

"Oh no, I would never ask you to," I assure. "I only ask that you describe me carefully."

Her brows knit. "Why would I have a need to describe you?"

I point to the trail leading up the slope of Mount Parnassus. "You will be asked who is destined to marry the hapless virgin coming to see you. And you know that I am to be the bridegroom, yes?"

She squares her shoulders. "Yes."

"As you announce me as her betrothed, describe me not as a god but as monster. Terrify them with tales of heartache and insanity that are the result of my work. Bid them abandon her on the rocky cliff overlooking the sea near her father's house, dressed as if to attend her own funeral."

"But why?"

"To drive the family far away. To keep the girl safely to myself."

The Oracle regards me with disdain. "You wish to keep her from your mother as well, boy."

Now it is I who falter. "I want to ensure our happiness away from parents who would not yield otherwise."

"You love this girl?"

"Yes."

"And will for all time?"

My heart swells. "Yes."

"Very well, I will do as you request." Yet before I can fly away she seizes my wrist to still me a moment longer. "Eros, there is a prophecy for you as well. Your love will die if she sees you in your true form yet will live forever if she survives. So, too, will your daughter. Remember this."

She lets me go and I stare at her, puzzling what her strange words might mean. I fly away knowing that my errand is through.

I can still hear my father and sisters wailing as they walk away. The ocean below me churns, and I wonder if it would be better to dive into the deep on my own accord than lie in wait for the savagery the Oracle foretold.

"Psyche shall wed the Almighty Monster, to whom men and gods alike are enslaved," she had intoned. "He who tears out hearts and consumes bodies with fire will be her husband for eternity."

Unwilling to weep, I decide to stand and wait. Even if my husband is murderous and fierce, I could yet escape, or tame his heart, or any number of things. Hope still lives.

All is quiet except for the shuddering waves below. A breeze comes from the west, teasing the hem of my robes, a wedding dress and shroud combined. Suddenly I am airborne, seated in the arms of two unseen men. I shriek, terrified that I will tip over and splatter on the rocks. An invisible hand steadies my shoulders as a voice whispers words of comfort.

"My lady, you are safe. We are taking you to your husband's home, now your home as well."

We float over olive groves and vineyards, tinged red and gold in the afternoon light, and I marvel at the sight. I have a thousand questions yet cannot speak, I am so overwhelmed. Soon I am on land once more, catching my breath and regaining my balance. The whispers resume, warm against my ear. "Welcome home, my lady."

I stand at the foot of an expansive set of white stone stairs leading up to a columned palace and must arch my head back to take in its vastness. Mosaics are beneath my feet, the love stories of gods and mortals wrought in jewels. Even though winter is approaching, spring flowers twist into canopies that dapple the sun across an immense terrace. Vases are as tall as trees; sculptures are as massive as giants. Mortal men could never do work this fine or this immense.

I am wed to an immortal. Perhaps a monster but more likely a god. Monsters would not care for such artistry.

Before my astonishment can turn to fear, I hear more whispering, a woman this time. "My lady," she says, her breath warm in my ear, "please come with me. We will see to your bath."

A light touch at my elbow guides me down a hall to a

bathing pool fed by ewers suspended in the air. Invisible hands help me undress, loosening my braids and guiding me into the water. I am seated by my unseen servant, who pours water over my head and rests my back against her body. She massages my scalp and combs my hair. It is soothing beyond measure.

"That feels wonderful. Thank you."

"I am yours to command, my lady." A pumice circles down one side then the other, scouring my back and shoulders, hands and feet. A sea sponge, dented by the grip of unseen fingers, rinses me off, and I am offered a hand to step out of the pool. She rubs oil into my skin that is infused with the seductive sweetness of lilies.

My old robes discarded, I am outfitted like a queen, with pearls being woven into my braids and intricate gold brooches pinning the shoulders of my chiton. I am guided to a great room and asked to sit alone at a table set with silver platters. Music surrounds me as do the scents of grilled lamb and warm bread. I am ravenous, and before I can ask my plate is loaded up. I take a floating wine cup out of the air, my fingers brushing the knuckles of a male servant who is no more visible than my bathing attendant had been. I thank Demeter and Dionysus and begin to feast.

Between bites I throw many questions out to the air: How many servants are in the household? Do you have names? Where is this palace in relation to my father's house? Who cooked this delightful meal so I may thank you? The servants whisper their answers, humbly refusing any thanks. But the real question goes without adequate answer:

"When will I meet my husband?"

"When it is time."

I am sated and sleepy. The familiar voice of the servant who drew my bath comes close to my ear, and I am led to a room set off from the rest of the palace. It is a bedchamber vivid with flowers and soft pillows, with a window facing the east framing the moon and stars. I am undressed for bed and as my servant wishes me good night, I drift off.

All day I have known she is there, waiting for me.

My aim has been off since this morning, my arrows whizzing past my intended targets. Mother cursed me as I restrung my bow again and again. My tasks seemed stupid and meaningless, plunging meager people into the depths of delight over those who were substandard when compared to her. As Helios' chariot hovered above, I considered shooting one of his stallions so he'd race across the heavens to find a mare to mount, dragging the sun away so I could hide myself in the darkening sky.

At last, the sun begins to set. Mother retires to her quarters—and off I fly.

I know she will be sleeping, her skin smooth with oils, her hair spreading across her bare shoulders like golden lace. She will be lying among the soft linens on the broad bed in the flower-strewn chamber I designed, set apart and

18

private, a place for us alone.

I alight at the window and there she is, curled beneath the covers, unaware of her power over me. I nearly tumble from my perch, my legs weak at the sight of her. I hold fast and wait a moment more.

As I have watched lovers discover each other time and time again, I have learned much. I have seen how rampaging lust clouds the mind and disposes of reason, while tenderness sharpens the senses and prolongs the joy. I know that two hearts choosing each other build the strongest bonds, and those who give pleasure get more in return. Thus I had no arrow for her, no sweet poison to thicken in her veins. She will be mine only if she wishes it, if she chooses me.

Remembering the Oracle's words of warning, I stay invisible as when I do my secret archery when I touch down at her bedside. The silk of her hair curls around my fingers. Her back, not burdened by wings, is a warm expanse, and I stroke downward, my palm coming to rest in the valley at the base of her spine. My lips touch her shoulder, my nose buries into the soft curve of her neck. She stirs, and I am quick to whisper, "Shh, all is well, my beautiful one."

She turns on her back, her arms shielding herself. Her eyes are full of alarm. "Who's there? I cannot see you."

I take her hand and hold it to my heart. "It is your husband, dear Psyche. Do not fear."

"Why can't I see you?"

I kiss her palm then lightly brush her cheeks with my lips. "It is my will."

Her perfume, lingering from her time in the bath, fills my nostrils as I taste the skin at her throat. She coos, relaxing into the bed, trusting my words and my touch. I kiss lower, nestling between her breasts. Her hands cup the back of my head, and she guides me to her nipple; my hands span under her, pulling her to me. Her voice is low, her arousal thickening the air as I ring her navel with a string of kisses. I breathe in her scent as I trace her pink petals with my tongue, coaxing nectar from her flower. She begins to crest and I guide her over the wave, my fingers within her, murmuring my love.

I lie beside her and gather her up, belly to belly, heart to heart. Her bliss still heavy in her eyes, she ventures to touch me, her fingers describing my form since sight cannot. When she brushes against feathers she freezes, the shock of the unexpected pulling her away from me. My heart stills, fearing she will flee.

"What is this?" she asks.

"Who I am."

"Let me touch you. Please, trust me."

I turn my back to her, trembling. Even invisible there would be no hiding my monstrousness from her touch. I watch her over my shoulder as she stretches her hands toward me without fear. She discovers the arch of bone and plumage rooted in my spine and curving toward my waist. She caresses their wide span, gentle and curious.

"So soft."

She touches every feather, stroking the sinews and contours of my wings, as Leda did when Zeus the swan claimed her. She sits astride the backs of my thighs then slides her body over my wings, her voice low and pleased as my feathers caress her. She nuzzles my neck, her sex against my buttocks, her breasts pressing into the down at my shoulders.

"Whether you are monster or god," she says, "you are wonderful."

I can take this torture no longer. Rolling her under me, my wings unfurl. We kiss, deep and hard. No honeyed words as I thrust within her, only animal sound. I have seen this act so often and curled my lip in disgust at the unseemly loss of control. Now I am here for the first time myself, overthrown by the passion that undoes mortals and gods, and she is all I could ever want.

She shudders and gives way. I follow, my body rigid then languid. I am panting as she settles into my arms, her blind kisses tasting the salt of our sweat mingled together. My wings fold over us, protecting us from the night's chill, keeping us close. Sweetness fills these moments: small kisses; light touches; words of care; words of lust. Our bodies long to learn more of each other, and throughout the night we acquiesce time and time again. Sleep draws over her like a blanket just before dawn, warm and peaceful.

As the sun's chariot begins its ascent, though, my heart grows heavy. I have to leave her. My work keeps the world fruitful and lively; without me it would wither. She will need to wait for me until night, and I will pine for her until then.

I wait for him all day, as I have done day after day.

I occupy myself with the loom and the lyre, but they barely distract me. I wave off the invisible servants so I may enter the kitchen and bake bread, for the homey smell of yeast and the ability to do something to fill the many hours. I walk the gardens, I arrange flowers, I watch the birds. There is not much else to do.

I starve for his company.

I despise the first light of day. He startles from our bed, sleep barely cleared from my eyes, and with a kiss he is gone. I believe he hoists a bow and quiver to his shoulders before departing; I have heard the rattle of arrows and the ringing of the string. He vows to return with the evening and always does. He keeps his word.

I imagine him constantly, for he remains unseen.

I know some things for certain. Other details I make up and believe to be true. His hair lies in waves against his brow; I imagine him dark-haired and fair-eyed, for those are my preference for a man. My fingers and lips have mapped his body. I can conjure the brave arch of his nose, the set of his jaw, the fullness of his mouth. His skin is smooth like a youth's; his stomach is lean; his chest is broad. We twine together at night, his legs with mine, and

I listen to his heartbeat.

He cannot be a monster: he has a heart.

Yet I have stroked the incredible arc of his wings, so he cannot be human.

Wings! Perhaps silver or gold, for he could well have wings of precious metal. No, they must be white; pure and soft, downy and warm against my skin. While I have not seen them stretched aloft, I know they are large, as my arms cannot span them.

What he is—who he is—remains a riddle.

I hear him as the day darkens: the beat of wings, the touch of his feet on the floor. He speaks my name and I respond.

"Husband."

The embrace is sweet. He cradles me against his body. I close my eyes, preventing my sight from distracting me in futile search for him in front of me as we kiss. I see his eyes, his form, his gentle smile, only because my eyes are closed.

I knead his weary shoulders, the tight backs of his calves, his slender feet. Hearing him sigh I imagine the contentment across his face. I touch and kiss and suck and lick. I take him in my mouth so carefully until his time comes near and he moans my name. He stops me so he can lay me beneath him then he moves within me. I close my eyes, imagining the sweat on his brow and the heat of his gaze as I break apart and come together again in his arms.

###

Psyche has stirred in me a change. When I first saw her and my arrow's tip drew my own blood, my heart ached. The silhouette of her body within her robes, the lock of hair that works itself free from the braid over her ear, her eyes dark and brimming with warmth—all of her myriad features attracted me closer.

It was desire for her body, yes, but also a desire to be near her, to look into her eyes and find peace and comfort. I set her on high in my palace to keep her shielded from others—Mother in particular—yet also to delight her and make her happy, for her smile brings me incredible joy. That aim—to please her enough for her to stay with me willingly—is what I desire most.

I want to know all of her: her memories, her pain, her turns of phrase, what makes her laugh. I want to ease her fears and ensure her safety and joy. I have never wanted to live so much for another. Perhaps that is what separates men from gods: that selflessness. Even after months with her at my side, each day affords me a novel discovery.

If Psyche can but follow one rule, she will be safe, and all will be well.

###

Our passion is taking a toll on my mortal flesh. These days I feel oddly sore and discomfited. The scent of wine in my cup makes me ill. I fall into a deep slumber in mid-afternoon. I am not myself.

During my long walk in the garden I remember that my sister, just married a few short months, took sick as I am. Her moods were changeable, her tastes strange. I murmured my concerns, and she laughed with the ring of an elder's superiority. "Silly little girl, this is what a woman is made for."

My heart skips. I think of the last blissful weeks in the arms of my beloved and what has to be true.

He is here now, I can sense it. His voice warms all parts of me.

"Psyche."

"My husband."

He pulls me close and as all nights, we fall under the sway of the song our bodies sing together. Yet as he traces my breast with the lightest of touches, I suck in my breath. He stops.

"Did I hurt you?"

"No, my love."

"What is wrong?"

"Nothing at all. I am with child."

I wish to see his face. I want to read it, know whether he is happy or scared, angry or ecstatic. All I can do is tune my ears to the small sound of a smile or frown forming on his unknowable face.

I hear a stagger of breath. "Oh," is all he can manage

before his kisses rain over me. Joy pours forth from us both in laughter and tears, yet I do not fully relax.

"Fair Psyche, this is wonderful news," he soothes. "Are you not happy?"

I start to cry. Through all the mystery, the unfamiliarity and strangeness of our union, I have stood fast and accepted all. Now I am crumbling and the tears cannot stop.

"What of our child?" I ask. "Will it be winged as you are, and tear at my womb? Will it be a beast—a boy with a bird's head or a girl with a bill and webbed feet?"

I fear he will leave me to unseemly weeping, disgusted and hurt, for what I say must surely wound him. Yet his words are soft. "Do not fear. The child will be beautifully built as you are and well loved by us both. She will—"

"She? You know this?"

His lips brush my ear, his voice shimmering in my soul. "Yes, our child is a girl."

My heart soars, imagining shiny curls and bubbly smiles. Then I falter. "Will she be invisible like you, with me never seeing her face or knowing the color of her eyes? Will she have a name I am allowed to speak, or will she be a cipher to me, as you are?"

Now he stills at my side, hesitating to speak. We talk of this often, his keeping himself hidden from me, and he has no answer I can accept for this. It is our one quarrel.

"Why must you stay unseen, my husband? Why are you still unnamed to me? What do you fear—that I will be consumed by the fire of your glory? That I cannot comprehend your power?"

"No."

"Are you hiding from someone? Do you fear that person's wrath if you are found out through me?"

"No more questions."

"Can you please trust me with your full self, now that I carry our child?" His silence angers me. "Why will you not trust me?"

"Trust is all I ask of you as well. Trust that this is for the best."

"But why?" I storm. "I have been obedient and patient over these many weeks, cut off from my family and alone with my thoughts for hours on hours. I must cadge chores from the servants so I have something to fill my time here. I ache for you in the daylight, I give myself over to you until dawn yet you keep this from me. Why?"

"Enough questions." He does not raise his voice when he speaks, and thus I lower mine. Anger will not budge him. Perhaps honest talk will.

I reach out and find his hand, placing it on my belly. "We must be guides for our daughter. We must show her that marriage cannot rely on secrets and true love comes from knowing all—the good and the bad—and still remaining true. This cannot continue. You must let me know your identity or we will be always apart, as strangers."

He strokes my stomach with his cheek. I thread my fingers through his hair, caressing and consoling. I hear him stand, and he brings me toward him. As I close my eyes, we kiss and I see him in my mind's eye, strong and gentle.

"My love," he says, "there are reasons beyond your understanding for what I do."

"I can understand much," I say, smiling as I tweak his ear.

"You are mortal."

"Yes, and still I can understand."

"Our child does not have to be. She can be born to be like the gods, eternally youthful and alive, with no fear of death or decay."

My mind tosses. "She will be a goddess?"

"Only if you continue to obey my wishes, Psyche. Only if I remain unknown to you in form and name."

"But why?"

He takes a moment to answer. "Because it is my will."

"And if I learn who you are, what of our daughter?"

"She will be born, and age and die, just as ... just as you will."

I mull this. My wishes for myself had been short-sighted: busying my days, waiting for my husband. Now the limitless future spans before me.

"Will I ever be immortal?"

"That is to be seen."

"So I will age while you and our child do not."

He does not answer.

My throat becomes tight. "And as youth is left behind, you will leave me."

"No."

"Why would you not? My beauty will fade, my body will fail. Your attraction to me cannot stand the barrage of time. Why would a youth want a crone in his bed?"

"I will not leave you."

"And our child, will she care for me in my dotage or will she, too, be absent from my days only to drift in the window as the sun sets?"

Tears come to my eyes again, which quickly I wipe away. He stops my hand and kisses the salt from my fingers. "My sweet, make no mistake: my secret is not to be questioned again. You must be content with how things are, for the sake of our marriage and the sake of our child."

He walks me to our bed and pulls the covers back; I imagine his hands turning the blankets as they seemingly move in the air, unaided. I am weary but fretful. His arms find their familiar circle around my shoulders and we nestle together. His touch is slow and circles down my back, and I sigh.

"I am nothing but my love for you," he whispers. "That is all I truly am. I am yours."

"And I am yours, my husband, and you are mine, as you are."

"What may I do for you?" she asks me.

"Nothing. You are all already."

"Do you have a favorite color?"

I had never considered this. "Why would you ask?"

"Perhaps I may weave a mantle to your liking, with embroidery, too. I have many fine talents you know not of."

"A mantle? To throw over my wings? How may I fly?"

She frowns. "I want to make something to show my love for you. I cannot conceive of what you might need, having all at your command."

I caress her cheek. "The baby is taking you over. You are like a duck feathering her nest."

She is not thwarted. "Perhaps this instead: may we dine together?"

"My sweet, I need no food."

"Need none, or want none? Can you not eat?"

"I have no need for bread or meat."

"But *can* you eat? If I were to make a dish for you, would you enjoy its taste? Would your stomach growl at its scent and be satisfied once it is full?" She hesitates. "Do you *have* a stomach?"

I laugh. "Food can pass my lips, yes. Wine, too, and I can enjoy them both. I simply have no need for them."

"I am a good cook. I cared for my father after my sisters left the house. I have many favorites you might enjoy."

"My servants bring you all you could need to eat. Why make the effort?"

"It would be a gift from me to you, creating something we can share in addition to our bed. Giving us time to talk and laugh and ponder as we savor the meat and the bread: that is what mortals do."

"And I must do more of what mortals do?"

"Yes, my love, for therein lies compassion. You could use the experience of mortality to better understand us frail creatures. You are mighty, sure, and you are wondrous, but you and your immortal kin often act without caring about the consequences."

"I am made to answer prayers and that is all. It is the mortals who must weigh the consequences. If they do not do this before they ask for divine intervention, I cannot help them."

"I am not so sure you are so hard of heart or resolve. You

must be moved by what you see. The stories you tell me night after night, they are full of heartache and hope. You would not care enough to share those tales were you not affected. That is a good thing, my love."

"I have not always been thus. You have changed me."

"What brought you to love me? Why me, husband?" Her eyes look toward my voice, unable to capture my gaze as I stay hidden from her. In the low light of the lamps they are honey-colored and lovely.

I sigh. "Your wondrous beauty."

"But there are many beauties, and many reasons women may be called beautiful."

I take her hands in mine, my thumb tracing the lines in her palm. "Your eyes caught the sunlight the day I first saw you. That sight captured my heart."

"What if, after a first night together, you would have thought my beauty a poor counterweight to my dreadful personality or dull brain? Would you have dropped me into the drink and flown away?" Her laugh is like a flock of newly fledged birds. It is delightful.

"No fear of that. Your loveliness is well matched by your wit and charm."

"It is fortunate you have charm yourself, husband. My eyes can be no guide to your handsomeness, and I have to judge you on your personality alone." She reaches for my face, and I lean into her hand. "That is the safer path: to love the person more than his or her appearance, for you have to live with a spouse for a lifetime while beauty alters and fades."

I kiss her palm. "Perhaps you should counsel those I encounter to think about how to use the love granted to them."

"Perhaps I will someday, but tomorrow I will cook a meal we can enjoy together. And tonight ..." She sucks the tips of my fingers, and my body thrums as if it were a string on a harp. I watch her, her blindness to my visage making her touch slow and careful.

"Of course." I speak in a whisper, I am so transfixed.

She kisses my wrist, and my pulse pounds. She curls against me, and I fly us up to the sanctuary of our bed. She unclasps the pins at her shoulders and loosens the cord at her waist. I cast my robe aside. Her kisses scatter across my chest, her hands find me. She guides me in, and words lose their meaning.

I am three months along, and I am miserable.

Nothing tastes as it should. I am weak and moody, and I can scarcely hold any food in my stomach before I retch it up again. Though my invisible servants are attentive, they are not resourceful. If I know not what to do, they cannot help me. They have no maternal knowledge and so cannot advise me or offer me counsel.

I know not if this time will pass or if I must prepare to die. I fret for the baby, fearing I am starving her in my womb.

My husband knows nothing of what to do—pregnancy is as new to him as it is to me—and although he has a mother he dares not ask her to come to my aid. His fear of her troubles me; perhaps therein lies his reasons for keeping his identity hidden.

I wish that my mother could come, but she left the world as I entered it. My sisters could perhaps lend me aid in her stead. Both took the role of mother for me as I grew up, counseling me as best they could. Now they are mothers themselves and married to doughty men. They could care for me, make me broth, help me through the day. They could give me news of my father and share my joy with him.

My husband shudders as I ask for them to visit me.

"They will not understand what we have together. They will be jealous."

"They love me."

"But they love themselves more. You are rare in humanity, my love. You came to this palace and saw not a trove of jewels to plunder and gold to sell, but a home to keep with your husband. You heard the disembodied voices of the servants and did not let fear overtake you; in fact you are kinder to them than most mistresses are with their human slaves. You received me into your bed with joy, despite how alien our union must be. Only one so refined as you could do so. Your sisters, I fear, are not so well-mannered."

"I love them."

"I do not fault you for that, but you must see them for who they are. I never saw them nor attended their first meetings with their betrothed. Thus they know not love in their marriages, which makes them greedy for what they do not have themselves. Their misery has made them cunning, I fear. They will sow seeds of doubt in your heart simply to ruin your happiness since they have none of their own."

"You say you do not know them. How are you so sure?"

"From how you describe your childhood it is not a great leap to assume this is true."

My shoulders square. "Husband, you have given me much, and I am grateful and humbled by your gifts. What you cannot give me is counsel on humanity. I am with child, and as she grows strong I grow weak. I need the strength of human company at a time like this. I long for my family. I know this is strange to you, but even if they are flawed, they are beloved by me. I want them here, and I beg you to grant me this one, first wish."

He sighs. "This will be the end of us, if they come."

"You cannot know that."

"Oh, but I do. I have seen it so often it makes my head whirl. Jealousy is a common and stealthy intruder in the matters of love. It is as inevitable as it is ugly, and it runs in families."

I begin to weep. This is the ploy of conniving wives of tenderhearted men, but plagued by fatigue and loneliness I cannot halt the tears. "I am sick and alone. I have no human to speak to for advice or aid, and I fear I may die of this child as my mother did of me. My sisters know me best and can care for me better than your phantom handmaidens. I need them by my side, even for a day, or I may be lost."

He brings me to his lap and strokes my hair. "My sweetest love, I can only beg you reconsider your wish, for their visit will set in motion our doom."

"I will be careful. I will watch for their snares. I promise, my love, if you do this for me all will be well."

I feel his shoulders lower, and he sighs again. Thus I know he has capitulated.

"I will order the West Wind to bring them to this place tomorrow."

My heart leaps. "Oh thank you, thank you, my beloved!" I drown his misgivings with kisses and soothe his fears with touch.

Each time we are together, I have kept invisible for both our sakes. The Oracle's prediction was dire: my love will die if Psyche sees me in my true form. I fear this means very sight of me will make her combust as Dionysus' mother did; the glory of a god can be too much for mortal eyes to withstand. I cannot tell her this. Her every breath would be labored by the priestess' dread prediction.

Yet I cannot stay unseen when I sleep. When we are

together, our bodies drifting off to sleep in a glow of spent passion, I am careful to let her fall under Lethe's spell before I do, and I rise before her eyes open. I have done this every night of our union, no matter how tired or spent I feel, because I fear the harm that will come her way otherwise.

If she is taken from me, my existence will be everlasting torture. I will live forever as a wraith, though my reason for living is gone. I will do anything to prevent this.

Why does she question me? I am her husband, her protector, a half of her whole. She would do well to follow my dictates rather than argue. She is fortunate: if I were another husband I would greet her questions with the back of my hand. If I were another god she would be cast aside and destroyed.

And yet ... and yet ... her sisters are here.

My sisters are not to blame. They did not sow doubt in my heart—that was already there—though they surely watered it.

Their eyes widened as they beheld the palace, so crafted that it was obvious human hands never cut the marble or shaped the silver or polished the jewels. I knew of what they whispered when they went to bed: how unfair it was that their marriages were to old men—whose purses and scrotums were by now equally empty—while their undeserving younger sister had wed wealth.

I know them well. They have harbored jealousy of me since I was a girl fetching attention from all quarters unasked. They make their dominion over me by questioning my reasoning. I have always trusted my intuition more than my looks to see me to happiness, so they chip away at my surety at every opportunity.

For all the knowledge of their true natures, still I wanted them at my side. I had hoped that time would bring them new perspective or mellowness, or that my pregnant state would strike some vein of tenderness in their hearts, but that was truly naïve. Instead their insidious questions echoed those I hid deep within me:

What kind of a husband forbids you to see him yet will not let you leave his presence? Why must he hide? What life can you have together if he cannot be known to you?

The Oracle said he is a monster, and it always speaks the truth. He must hide his true nature because he is sly and bewitching.

He is kind to you now yet will leave when he has his prize of progeny. He is powerful and will take your daughter. You will be left alone to die.

You do not see it because he has disguised himself, but his true nature will come forth when he sleeps. Take your lamp and a knife to your chamber once he's deep in slumber and see him for who he is ... then take his life.

They prodded me to kill him. I would do no such thing ... yet if he has bewitched me all this time and truly is a monster I must protect myself and the daughter I carry. The knife feels heavy and cold in my hands.

He asked me to trust a silly rule out of abject obedience. In his place of privilege he could not comprehend the need for me to know all without restriction. I have to know. He just can never find out.

I gather my lamp and my knife and enter our room, as I have without question for many months. I stand by the bed and raise the light. As the glow illuminates our bed, I understand the gravity of my mistake.

His face is golden in the lamplight, his hair dark and soft. He is a sturdy youth with graceful limbs and noble features. His skin is smooth and unblemished; his cock sleeps between his legs. His feathery wings fan around his shoulders, glowing white. At his feet lay the bow and quiver I had supposed he owned. They bear the imprint of Hephaestus and so must be godly in manufacture and purpose. I slide an arrow out of the quiver and its tip across my hand to see it up close. It is sharp and painful. I watch a cut open and mend in my palm and I grow dizzy.

Nervously I cast my eyes on my husband to see if my sounds have wakened him, and I am overwhelmed by desire. This creature, so handsome and vulnerable, is all I want.

I know my husband's name, for he is Love himself.

Eros.

Even as he sleeps I am desperate for forgiveness. I understand his distrust of human resolve, for he has seen thousands of us lie and cheat and desert those who love us for no better reason than the fact that we can.

I stagger. A drop of oil is loosed from the lamp and sizzles as it hits his shoulder. My beloved husband rears up, howling with pain. He casts around for the source of the injury. When he meets my eyes, his become dark and sad.

"Without trust there can be no love."

With an awful beating of wings he is gone, as are the walls around me. Our home disappears and I spin and land in the dirt on the hillside, on all fours like a pitiful animal. When I at last take in a breath, it leaves as a scream.

Within my grief is abject terror. I know of no story where it is fortunate to be loved by the gods. Women like me, who have spurned immortal advances or angered one of Olympus' residents, do not live long or well. Ask Daphne, now Apollo's favored tree. Seek Callisto, turned into a bear and then into stars. Dionysus' poor mother was reduced to ash; Athena's wise mother was swallowed by Zeus. A pitiful woman like me has little chance for long life or peaceful death. Nor does my child, now that her mortality is set.

I come to a river, deep enough to lie in, its cold water a ready shroud. I step in and fall back, my arms outstretched like my lover's wings. The current carries me swiftly and I sense my doom will come from breaking apart on the rocks, when suddenly I find myself on shore. It was as if strong hands had pushed me back on my feet, well away from the danger. I see no one, though the reeds hiss a rebuke.

Psyche, death is not your fate. You must hope. You must find a way back to him.

My womb echoes that message as my daughter quickens within me. When my own life is not enough reason to continue, hers must be.

If Eros will not see me, I will find Aphrodite and beg her to intercede. It is the only way.

I fly far from the palace, putting swift distance between me and my impulsive rage. I do not get far. The wound to my shoulder is the first I have ever suffered, save the scratch that condemned me to love. Though the burn is small, the pain is deep and overwhelming. I drop to the ground, exhausted and ashamed.

I am a fool for loving a mortal so much.

Psyche's failing is optimism, believing her sisters could change their natures as snakes shed their skins. Those sisters: vipers in the rosebushes. How they share the same blood as benevolent Psyche is beyond my understanding. They are to blame for our love's destruction. Their jealousy feasted on our joy and doomed their sister to death when immortality was in her grasp. I would that I had my stepfather Ares' appetite for mayhem and blood. I wish to see them suffer. I want them dead.

I hear a rustling in the grass ahead. Standing before me is an immortal whose vestigial beauty is twisted and scaly. Her eyes are narrow and rimmed with blood; her wings are leathery and tipped with brutal talons.

"Tisiphone?"

"Eros, I am surprised you admit to knowing my name."
She flaps toward me and lands close to my crouching
form. "You called for me?"

"I spoke not a word."

"But you prayed for vengeance, did you not? That is the
prayer I am compelled to answer." She scuttles closer, her
breath foul. "We Erinyes are made to torment mortals for
their misdeeds."

"Do not go near Psyche, I warn you."

"No fear of that, oh soft and gentle Eros," Tisiphone
hissed. "I am here to bargain with you. I give you my oath
that your beloved's two sisters never threaten your union
again."

The favors of the Erinyes cut two ways. "What do you
demand of me?"

"I ask but one favor: a mate. There is one for everyone, is
there not? Why, monsters more hideous than I have had
litters of offspring. It is not as if I ask for the impossible."

My lip curls in disgust. "Who would you desire?"

"Deimos. I think we would make a well-matched pair:
Ares' son charging through the battlefield with me at his
side, Terror wedded to Vengeance." She sneers with
delight. "We would be step-kin then, fair Eros, though I
would never admit to having such a mooning youth for a
brother-in-law."

Her talons perch on my shoulder, her mouth close to my

ear. "Just think: with one arrow from your quiver, you will slay three hearts. That of my beloved, who will soon find kinship in my embrace—and those of the devious sisters who have massacred your happiness."

Blind with hatred for those women who call Psyche sister, I do not hesitate. "Do it. I will fulfill my promise in due time. Yet if Psyche learns of this, or comes to any harm because of you, you will suffer."

"Agreed." Tisiphone's smile is a gash, her laughter a shriek. "I know how I will do the deed. I will go to the elder one and adopt the voice of poor Psyche, crying and rending her garments. 'Dear sister,' I will wail, 'my husband took one look at you and has spurned me to be by your side. He is Eros, Sex Incarnate, and he wants nothing more than to make you the queen of his bed. Just jump from the cliff, and the West Wind will guide you back to him.' Only there will be no wind, only a long fall to a rocky death. What's done to one sister, I'll next do to the other. Then your revenge is complete."

Her ugly wings rise above her. "Do not forget your promise to me." She swoops toward the shore where Psyche's envious sisters reside, unaware of how their greed will become their doom.

Revenge does not mend my shoulder or my heart. I struggle into the air, gritting my teeth as I fly toward my mother's palace to recover, assuming I can.

Mount Olympus is miles ahead, fixed like a beacon. I walk

toward it, my daughter making my stomach uneasy, until the day is late. I must find shelter.

I come to a squat altar surrounded by broken shocks of wheat and small statues of maids holding baskets of grain. It was built as a dwelling place for Demeter on earth but in the ensuing years has become overrun and disrespected.

My piety mingles with the practical need to seek the counsel of those who know my lover's mother well. I find new grain and bind it together. I right the fallen statues and clean the leaves and debris from the columns. I lower my head to the ground and rededicate the space to the fair Goddess of the Harvest, asking her to bless the mortals in her care.

When I rise I see a woman, big bodied and lovely, though her face is marked with concern. "My dear Psyche, thank you for making this place holy again. But look at you, hungry and exhausted. You must eat."

In her hands appear a sack full of bread, figs and dates. I am so starved I nearly lunge at her but my sickness returns and my gorge rises at the mere thought of food. I keep my eyes lowered. "Thank you so much, madam, but I am not hungry."

"Is that child you're carrying making you ill?" she asks, placing the food on the altar and handing me a jar. It is warm to the touch. I open it and smell strong tea, fragrant with citrus.

"Ginger root and lemon. It will help settle your stomach." I swallow and feel balanced again. She smiles. "Now, nothing would please me more than to see you eat."

I feast until I am full. She watches me like a doting mother; I bow my head like a thankful child. She strokes my cheek.

"I know of your plight and your upcoming battle with Aphrodite, who is in an awful fury over her wounded son."

"Wounded? Has his shoulder worsened?"

"It is not his shoulder but his heart. He pines for you, cries your name hour after hour, declaring he was wrong and pleading for your forgiveness."

My heart leaps. "I must go to him."

"Not yet," the gentle goddess says, her restraining hand on my shoulder. "You may stay here for the night to sleep, and no harm will come to you on the journey ahead. But be forewarned, I cannot promise you that safety when you are at Aphrodite's mercy. Even we Olympians cannot cross her."

Once more she smiles at me with a mother's fondness. "I will help you any way I can." She points to the sack of food. "Keep this with you. It will replenish throughout your journey."

I fall to my knees in gratitude as she turns toward her mountain home. Before she leaves she provides a final blessing.

"May you be reunited with your love, for the joy of reunion almost makes the separation worthwhile."

Behind the altar is a barn, dry and well sheltered. I pull together straw and bed down for the night. My dreams are comforting, and I wake believing I am in Eros' arms, so glad I am home.

"*Psyche*?" I could not tell if Mother was laughing in her rage or raging in the midst of laughter. "Was there no nymph, no naiad or other immortal—no other creature on earth—to catch your eye instead of that ignoble human? Oh for the love of Zeus, stop crying or I'll never let you out!"

I came to Mother's tower chamber for her to tend my wounds and help me return to my wife's good graces, and yet she refuses to show me any sympathy. My agony over my impulsive mistake will not disappear. Each time I feel I've exhausted my tears another wave of grief takes me over. I burble Psyche's name and bury my face in the cushions on Mother's couch. She hurls a pillow at me and continues to fume.

"If you had done as I had asked, she would be trying to mate with a toad, and you would be much better off and back to work. Why do you want her after she has disobeyed you anyway? Let her starve or be torn apart by wolves. That's what she deserves, not your mewling and begging. Eros, be a man, not a browbeaten child—and STOP CRYING!"

Forgiveness is a profound irritation for my mother because she is unable to master it. At times I believe she is becoming more like her husband Ares with each passing day, enjoying the rages and rancor more than the harmony and tenderness the humans assign to her.

"Psyche was right all along," I wail. "It was wrong to hide myself and not share the reason for my secrecy. No wonder her sisters could sway her so easily. I am to blame!"

"I can stand no more of this!" Mother storms. "Until you can see reason here you will stay, and I will seek my peace at Olympus." The door slams and the bolt clanks into place. I am imprisoned. The tower is tall with a window far above me, too far for me to fly in my wounded state, even if I had the strength after weeping for so long.

I scream the only word that offers me comfort and hope.

"PSYCHE!"

The gates of Olympus rise in front of me. Three fair goddesses stand at the entrance: the Horae, sisters who guard the hours of the day and the seasons of the year. They amuse themselves by turning blossoms to fruit to falling leaves as I approach. I prostrate myself, knowing all I have to protect me is humility.

"Fair ones, I am Psyche, wife of Eros. I wish an audience with his mother, the Goddess of Love and Beauty. Please let me enter."

"Rise." Dike steps ahead of her sisters, approaching me with wonder. "Brave mortal, you will be entering the lion's den of a mother's rage. What do you hope to gain?"

"My husband."

The sisters look at one another with eyebrows raised. "You broke your vow to Eros," Dike intones. "You burned him with oil. Why not apologize to him?"

"Even if he chooses to speak to me I must first assuage his mother."

"You will be at her mercy," Eunomia says. "You will be given any number of trials designed to kill you or drive you to madness."

I stand tall. "It is what I must do. Else I will live in fear."

Eirene steps toward me. "May you find peace at the end of your journey."

The goddesses step aside, and the golden gates open. Sick with dread, I step into the hallowed palace of the almighty ones. I soon come to a room with twelve grand thrones circling a hearth. The thrones are empty, all but one.

"So you are the disease that has infected my son."

Even terror cannot stop my wonder. Aphrodite is what the blue sky is to birds or the rain to a garden. She is all that a mortal craves. To be in the presence of all that Love is—tenderness, jealousy, nurture, wantonness, utter beauty—stops my breath.

Quickly I move to bow before her. Quicker still, she grabs my hair and pulls me upright, her face devoid of softness or pity. "There is no word you can say that can save you, Psyche. My son has done nothing but wail and weep since you injured him. He cannot go on his rounds, so love cannot spark. Marriages cannot be consummated and babies cannot begin. The poet sits idle, and the musician stares at his lyre. No creation can take place because you have broken him apart!"

I fear she will pull my hair out by the handful. I look away from her sea-green eyes, dark with fury. "Please release me," I gasp. "Tell me how I can make this right."

She pushes me to the floor. "He has disobeyed me because of you. He and I are divided, with you in the middle. There is no place for you while you live!"

I cower on the stones. Her foot connects with my spine, and pain shoots through me like a sword. Desperate I cry out, "Don't kill me, for I bear your son's child, your granddaughter!"

Aphrodite groans. A moment before she is rage personified, and now when I look up she is weeping, rage and sorrow fueling her tears. "Eros, what have you done? A bastard who is half-mortal? Why would you disobey me so?"

I stand, her condescension needling my pride. "She is no bastard. We are husband and wife. Ask him yourself if you do not believe me."

"Silence!" The tears stop and the fury returns. "He has made an incredible error in judgment, and you must pay the price for his idiocy ere you may see him again. Your child has saved you for the moment, but when I return, mark me: you will suffer."

###

"She is with child? You fathered a *bastard*?"

I have never seen Mother in such a rage. She lashes out at me, snarling like a lioness. Sitting on a low bench nursing my enflamed shoulder, I can barely ward off her blows to be able to speak.

"She is my wife."

"No ceremony, no family by your side to witness your vows, no blessing from Hera and Zeus—no, she is *not* your wife, stupid boy! She is your concubine—your dreadful, human concubine!" She cuffs me on the head once more.

"That is easily fixed," I protest. "We will have a wedding feast at once … if she will only allow my return." At the thought of being bereft of her, tears thicken my voice and I am overcome with wailing, pleading to the Four Winds to tell Psyche of my contrition.

"Stop that insane noise!" Mother paces in the chamber, ready to rend her own clothes in frustration. "You do not even know what marriage means, what sacrifices it entails."

"I will gladly promise Psyche my loyalty and my love for all time."

"That is because your experience is narrow, your options untested. Unwed, you may play as you like, with whatever nymph or maid catches your fancy. Once you are married, though, that bond is holy." She raises her finger at me as if I am still a toddler. "Woe to the one who breaks that vow."

This taps an anger I did not know I possessed. "What vows have you kept, Mother? How many half-brothers and sisters of mine walk the Earth despite the marriages you have had? How many mortals have you sullied? How many gods have you betrayed? How dare you speak to me of marriage!"

Her lovely face goes ashen. "Who are you now, Eros? What has that mortal done to bewitch you? How will I bring an end to this?"

Her color quickly returns, followed by a wicked smile. "I have not the means to kill her without harming the child, but if she kills herself or goes mad, I may intervene. All I must do is drive her over that edge."

I struggle to my feet. "Mother, you will do no such thing."

"Stop me if you can, my wounded bird. She is my slave until she meets my demands."

She departs, full of black purpose. I spy the window, stories above my head. My wings spread as I try to catch the air, but I am too weak.

I cannot save Psyche without outside aid. I call to the winds but they do not respond. I spy the sun out the window but it would be pointless to ask Helios to abandon his chariot. No help will come from the air, and none but my mother knows I am kept here, imprisoned.

I collapse to the floor, injured and wretched. An ant creeps past me, aiming for an unseen tunnel, a lone messenger going out into the world. My anguish makes me latch onto a crazed idea. I crawl after it.

"Wait!"

It stops at a crack between stones as if ready to listen.

"Ant, please find my beloved Psyche. If you can lend her aid, I beg you to do all you can."

The insect marches onward and out, and for the first time in what seems like days, I sleep. Morpheus is kind to me and salves my tear-stained mind with lovely dreams, images of hope and beauty.

Psyche is asleep in our bed, swathed in linen. She wakes as I approach and lights from within when I touch her. She addresses me by name, her eyes joyous. She smells like spring, fresh and fecund. The moment we kiss I am deep within her, delighted and comforted to be one with her again.

She is a petty mistress, Aphrodite. This task has no purpose other than to drive me mad with despair.

A great pile of mixed seeds looms to my left. If it is sorted by this evening so Aphrodite can feed her doves with it, I will see another day.

I have been at this all morning and afternoon, yet the bowls are practically empty with barely a few dozen seeds covering the bottoms. My eyes well up as I envision my own funeral, then I command myself to focus because crying will get nothing done.

The drudgery makes my mind wander. I wonder what she will do to me while her kin grows within me. Shackle me to a tree until I give birth before becoming part of the forest? Turn me into a brooding hen until my daughter hatches then turn me into dinner? At least the girl will live, freed from her mother's plight to be cared for by her tender father. The mere thought of my baby in my beloved's arms brings tears back to my eyes.

Before I can weep, an army of ants swarm over the floor, their antennae vibrating. Exhausted as I am, the hum of their bodies seem to mimic words that bring me comfort.

Your burden is our pleasure, fair Psyche.

The insects cover the mound of millet and lentils, rice and wheat. Within minutes, the wooden sorting bowls fill as each tiny laborer drops its load and returns for more. Their rescue mission ended, they disappear.

I vow to never kill an ant again, and I will teach my daughter the same.

"That blasted Demeter!"

Mother rarely bothers to speak of the goddess of the harvest, who she considers to be a bumpkin unworthy of her concern. I listen with interest.

"Just because my first test had to do with grain, she sends insects to do the labor from her."

"What labor?"

"Sorting a pile of seeds. It would have taken the girl weeks and yet in the space of an hour it was done. But I am onto the source of her success: I saw a trail of ants leaving the chamber."

I recall my demented conversation with the insect the day before. "You are certain Demeter did this?"

Mother throws a pillow across the room in disgust. "She believes Psyche is a pious girl who deserves my love rather than rancor, just because she did a slave's job of tidying some rustic altar of hers. I am sure that weedy goddess had a hand in this. Who else could have?"

My joy brings me to my feet. "It matters not how she did it. Psyche has passed your test. You will release her to me now!"

"Oh no, I have not finished with her yet. I have another test at the ready, one that will not be so easy to survive. She cannot earn you back so easily."

My blood flares hot. "You cannot harm her, or I will never do your bidding again."

Mother eyes me. "Do not be so sure, my darling. Your brief dalliance is no match for our eternal bond." She nabs a crystal flask off a table top and steps lightly to the door. I step ahead of her.

"What are you doing?"

"Aphids are devouring the roses in my garden," she replies

with wicked glee. "Perhaps some water from the Styx will dispatch them once and for all. How fortunate that I know someone to run this errand for me." She dodges me and locks the door behind her. I am once again powerless to prevent the mortal danger lying in wait for my love.

I can fly higher than before but still I falter before reaching the window. My tears flow in frustration and anger at a mother who had been so loving to turn so cruel.

I look to the sliver of sky the window and see an enormous eagle. He serves Zeus, his reconnaissance keeping tabs on the world when the lord of the gods is occupied elsewhere.

Spending so much time in the sky has left me conversant with many birds, particularly those who serve Olympus. I call for him with an eagle's piercing cry. He circles back and wings down to perch on the back of a chair. I bow to him in greeting.

"Noble bird, I have a favor to ask."

He shrieks. "Why would I grant you one, after all the grief my master suffers due to your arrows?"

"Because it will be a way for Zeus to settle a score with my mother. If you do this for me I am certain it will pain her deeply." I stare into his shiny eyes. "Are you ready to listen?"

The eagle nods.

###

The crystal flask rests in my palm, the size of an apple. Tiny vial or huge vat, it would matter not. This task is impossible.

I will have to go to the maw of Hades and collect the water of the Styx. It is a pointless errand, for what use would Aphrodite have with the water?

My daughter moves within me and distracts me from my fear. I have spent so many months imagining the countenance of her father, I can easily imagine her face as well: eyes as blue as Eros', hair wavy and wheaten like mine; my father's broad smile, her grandmother's winsomeness. I wish I could cuddle her small, warm body to my breast, taking comfort in knowing I am no longer alone. I see no such comfort ahead of me.

I finish my meal, provided by dear Demeter's gift, and find my way down from Olympus toward the entrance to the Underworld.

When it comes into view I am astonished to find a great waterfall, gushing from hundreds of feet above into the swift, terrible river. The brambles are thick along the shore, and even with a sharp scythe I would not be able to reach the water before it disappeared into the cavern leading to the place where the dead receive their judgment. Instead I would have to wend my way to the top of the ridge where the water pours forth to fill my crystal flask. Frantically I search for a path to take me there, or a means of scaling the cliff's side, but find none.

Were my husband at my side he could fly to the top of the falls and fulfill his mother's demand. Were he able to reason with his mother, or defy her, perhaps I would not be here now, unprotected and desperate. My heart constricts, wishing for nothing more than a glance from him to let me know he is well.

A bird circles overhead and dives toward me: a giant golden eagle, fierce-eyed with ebony talons. It lands on an outcropping of rock and cocks its head, spying my flask. I clutch it tighter, fearing the bird will steal this glittering prize and I would be unable to fulfill my task, if even I could find a way to do so.

Fierce and magnificent, the eagle stares at me. Its cry pierces the air and I cower at the sound. His mighty voice turns human, and my heart stops:

Your beloved is more powerful than even my master Zeus, and I am obliged to follow his command. Give me the flask.

No longer surprised by mere talking animals, I reply. "My husband? How is he? Has he recovered?"

The eagle's noble head juts one way then another as if I am foolish to waste time.

The flask. Give it to me.

I hold it out and the massive talons surround it. Off he flies to the top of the heinous waterfall, holding it under the flow, careful not to be spattered by the spray. He swoops overhead again, circling down to a level where I can take it back again. I am without words beyond a feeble offer of "Thank you."

The eagle soars. His voice, piercing and awful, is yet

comforting.

Your love will hold you in his arms soon.

I am convinced this must be the last of the labors and my love will be at his mother's side when I return. Returning to Olympus on foot is no trouble. I am so happy, I feel as if I am flying on my lover's wings.

Mother is splayed across her bier, a cold compress over her eyes, vowing to "send that girl to Hell until she stays there." I smile with pride that my lady has bested the odds and has lived another day.

I am no more free than before. In fact, I am in yet more danger.

Her holy brothers and sisters sit on their thrones, many voicing their sympathy for me at Demeter's behest, yet Aphrodite still brims with vengeance.

"You have had supernatural help, mortal, and what sort of test of your mettle is that? I decree that no longer will the birds of the air or beasts on the ground give you succor. You must walk this next journey yourself, without aid along the way."

Then she describes my final labor and my blood runs cold.

Back to the mouth of Hades I must go. This time, I must enter to meet the Queen of the Underworld. My vainglorious mother-in-law says she requires a bit of her beauty to recover from her toil in caring of her wounded son.

There be but no way to enter but to die, I am certain.

Fearful as I am, I stand tall before her. "What of the child, the daughter of Eros I carry? Will you keep her safe as you refuse to do the same for me?"

Hera, Queen of Olympus, rises from her throne, her voice aflame with fury. "Aphrodite, you cannot endanger a mother-to-be. This is unholy. You do not want to brawl with my husband over this."

Zeus' grand throne sits empty, a fact which Aphrodite makes much of.

"Brawl, my fine madam? It is more likely that Zeus and I will share a laugh over a cup of wine instead. I am not afraid of your threats when he and I have so long a relationship."

Before the cuckolded goddess can descend on Aphrodite, Demeter intervenes. "Psyche does not have to die. She but needs to pay the ferryman and feed the fearsome guardian at Hades' palace door. Then she may come and go unharmed. Am I right, fair Aphrodite?"

Suddenly sulky, Aphrodite nods. Demeter is at my side.

"Come with me. I will give you what you need."

She wraps two wheat cakes soaked in wine in a piece of linen. "One cake will satisfy three mouths. Use one as you enter and save one for when you leave, and Cerberus will not harm you. You also need payment for Charon. Hephaestus?"

The master of the forge comes to us, and I am glad I am no longer easily surprised. In a palace where all the immortals are beautiful and proud, he is misshapen and bowed. His face is bronzed by many fires, his hands knobby and calloused. His body lists to one side, and his legs are scarred. Yet his voice is as warm as his countenance is rough.

"Madame, hold these coins dear. One will get you passage over the Styx, the other will get you back again. You will also need this." He limps to his throne and picks up an ornate box, which he places in my hands. "For Persephone to fill."

"Many thanks, kind sir."

The craftsman's smile is as crooked as his legs. "It is my pleasure to serve true love's purpose." He squeezes my hand then hobbles back to his place.

Demeter walks with me to the gates of the palace. As they open she looks over her shoulder to ensure no others overhear her instructions. "Tell my daughter you have my favor, and she will do whatever you ask." With a wistful sigh she adds, "And tell her I miss her more with each passing day."

She kisses my cheek, and I depart.

###

Mother is in my cell again, attempting to be conciliatory.

"Do you remember when I found you, a storm of energy and power with no form? I promised to guide you, give you purpose, make you worthy of awe. Mothering you is not always a happy task."

I stay silent, taunting her with furious quiet. She sits on a couch close enough to touch the top of my head if I would let her. She continues, undeterred.

"You are angry with me now, but soon you will accept the wisdom of my actions."

I say nothing. Answering her would give credence to the idea. Her voice is gentle and maternal.

"Humans must know their place in the universe. They are to revere us, to follow our directives with humility, to stay where they are put. Without praise and obedience, gods and goddesses have no worth. We Olympians would disappear without their worship. Our stories would be meaningless, our gifts wasted. How could the world be as wondrous if the fearful gods are not the cause?"

"It will be wondrous as long as Psyche is in it."

"She was wrong to turn you against me," she says. "I was wise to end this dalliance since you could not. And if it comforts your love-addled heart, her story will make her a heroine for the ages: the mortal girl who died traveling to Hades to prove her love for a god."

I scramble to my feet. "Died?"

"I expect Charon is paddling her down the Styx as we speak and few make a return trip. Son, she is as sure as dead."

Dead. The shock hollows me like a statue of bronze, immovable and cold. Fury dries my tears before they are shed, now that I know the aim of my mother's treacherous jealousy. My mind takes an ugly turn.

I place my hand on her shoulder and smile, my words dripping with contrition. "Mother, how wrong I have been to displease you and how right you were to slay the girl. You have given my work new clarity of purpose. Where is your husband?"

The question catches her off guard. "He is with the Trojans. Why do you ask?"

"Bring him here. I wish to see him."

"You have never exchanged even a passing word with Ares. Why must you meet him now?"

"While we may not have spoken—if he even can speak, for all I hear from your bedchamber are roars and grunts—I know he covets my arrows. He wishes to add them to his arsenal and, as a show of my capitulation to you, I will be glad to give them to him."

Mother is uneasy. "He has all the machines of war at his disposal. Why would he need something as paltry as a quiver of arrows?"

"Consider, Mother, what would happen if the God of War dispatched all the arrows of Desire. Rape … desecration …

bloodlust … unspeakable violation. These are rare perversions of normal order now, but what if they became the way of the world, the only way desire could be expressed?"

"Ares would suck the harmony and compassion out of love and sex like marrow from a bone, and you know it."

"When he does you will be powerless to stop him, for I will be nowhere to be found. I would be far from you, mourning forever the loss of my Psyche, the last light of love that humanity had ever seen—the light you extinguished."

"You could not do this," she whispers, fearful and pale.

"You leave me little reason not to. You say my love is dead, so all love should die with her."

She bolts past me, panicked. "I will see you locked in this cell for eternity before letting this happen. I will get the chains Hephaestus crafted for Prometheus' bondage and wrap you with them until you barely breathe!"

I hear the door lock behind her and only then do I collapse, my rage ebbing and sorrow flowing in. I keen for Psyche, begging the winds to turn me to dust so I will feel no more pain, no more loss.

Two doves flutter into the chamber, small baskets dangling from their mouths. They place their burdens on the floor then hop toward me, cooing words of comfort.

Sweet Eros, there is no time for despair. Psyche will soon emerge from Hades, alive and freed from your mother's control. Demeter has arranged it.

The birds alight on my hands, cooing still.

Eat what we have brought. It will heal you and permit your escape.

They fly out the high window toward Olympus. Within my heart, hope flickers once again. I take up the baskets and find within nectar and ambrosia. Tasting the food of the immortals, I am renewed. I test my wings and they bear me easily. I soar out the window, off to reunite at last with my fair Psyche.

"You don't smell dead."

Charon is crouched and craggy. He looks me over and sniffs as if I were a fish at the market and grunts.

"Got the fare?"

I hand him a coin from Demeter's bag slung over my shoulders. He sniffs again.

"Don't need no food where you're going."

"It's not for me, sir."

Shrugging, the boatman lends me a hand and I sit on the low seat. The Styx is dark in the cave's dim light. I had braced myself to see the mournful shades of the dead, and they pace in the distance. Yet I had not prepared for their ceaseless, piteous groaning. It is not frightening. It is woefully sad. They pine for children left behind, spouses yet living, parents who weep still on earth above after burying their child too soon. My heart, heavy with my own separation and loss, nearly breaks.

The boat pulls up to a dock and Charon struggles to help me onto shore.

"Where is the palace of Hades and his fair bride?" I ask.

He points a crooked finger. "There. Past the dog."

Before I see it I hear it snarling. I jump back, my eyes fixed on the snapping jaws two short paces away. Its heads strain from a body the size of a doorway, savage and starving. My hands shake as I remove the linen packet from my bag and unwrap it. I toss a cake toward the nearest of the mouths, and as it takes flight the other one falls to the ground. I snatch it up just before the growling mouths can feast on it. The first head bolts the cake down its gullet, and soon the beast is snoring and harmless.

Saying a prayer of thanks to Demeter I leave the sleeping creature and enter the palace. The shady servants scatter as I walk past, so I walk unaccompanied toward a room that by its size and décor has to be the queen's quarters. I stop at the threshold and call out softly.

"Dread queen, may I enter?"

"Come."

She stands at a window, beautiful as a flower encased in frost, her bright colors muted, her blue eyes steely, her golden hair silvery in the gloom. I lower myself to the floor and bow, my words cast before me like a shield.

"Persephone, doleful Queen of Hades, I am Psyche. I bring a message from your mother. She sends you her unending love and longs to see you at her side."

"You have spoken to my mother?" The joy rattles in her throat, as if her happiness has been caged and neglected in this woeful place.

"Demeter has become my patron. I owe her much and bless her name."

"Rise." Her eyes search mine. "You are yet alive. Why do you come to the land of the dead?"

"I am on an errand so that I may be reunited with my true love."

"If he has died there is naught to be done. Death makes no bargains."

"No, madam, he is immortal yet his mother keeps me from his side."

"And she is?"

"Aphrodite."

Persephone's brow furrows. "Your beloved is the winged archer?"

"Yes."

"Love has found love?"

I touch my stomach. "Yes, we are making a life together." I hold out hope that even in this dire place, Persephone may be like her mother, warm and maternal, and willing to aid a woman with child by granting her wish. Yet her face grows cold.

"Hades fixed his eye on me when Eros' arrow drove deep into his dark heart. Had he not aimed so true, I could be with my mother above in eternal sunshine, perhaps delighting in my own child's laughter and smiles. Yet here below I will never conceive, even if I wanted to bear my loathsome husband's heir. How can a life begin in a place of death?" Her eyes wet, she turns away. "I am of no mind to do Eros any favors."

I look away from her, my eyes cast down, desperation driving my bravery. "I am terribly sorry, madam. While your sorrow is your own, I understand your anguish. Yet if your mother's patronage can hold any sway, I beg that you do me one small service."

"And what is that?"

"Aphrodite requests some of your beauty. If it pleases you, gaze into this box then I will depart and pain you no more." I hold out the box, praying to Demeter that her daughter will thaw enough to show me a kindness.

The Queen of the Underworld sighs then takes the casket from me. "For my mother's sake, I will do as you request."

She completes the task, shutting the lid tightly. "This should be more than enough to satisfy Aphrodite's appetite for beauty." Then for the first time she offers me a smile. "In fact, there is enough for you both. After your travails you will want to slough off the weariness of the journey before you see fair Eros again. When you return to Olympus, open the box a crack and let my gift do its magic for you as well."

Handing over the box, the queen turns away from me. Her eyes look upward through the window as if she searches for a crack in the vault of hell through which to escape.

I thank her and take my leave: past the horrific dog, who gobbles a second wine-soaked cake and slumps, then to Charon's landing where I exchange my coin for passage away from the moaning and sorrow. Back to the living, back to the light, back to my love.

Upon seeing me the Horae open the Olympian gates and in I go, my steps light and my head held high. I stand in the hall just outside the throne room, grateful my long journey is done and my labors complete. I wipe sweat from my brow with the back of my hand. The intricate braids from my time in Eros' castle have unraveled and tangled, and I am footsore and smudged with dirt. As I am hardly presentable for the immortals in the next room, I am grateful to gracious Persephone for providing a balm for me as well as my former mistress.

I barely open the casket and palpable gray smoke slips out and wafts over my face. As I breathe in the vapor, I choke. My head rings with the sound of a wailing girl pleading for mercy from her awful husband, his violent lust extinguishing her innocence and her freedom all at once. Persephone's despair constricts my heart and withers my spirit, and all goes black.

###

Wherever my mother is, my beloved cannot be far from her. I fly toward the hallowed Olympic palace and swoop over the gates into the front hall.

There is a bundle of cloth on the floor near the entrance to the throne room. As I alight I see it is a woman, her hand resting on a jeweled box.

My heart drops to my stomach.

"Psyche?"

A thick web clouds her face. I pull its awful tendrils from her mouth and nose, calling her name again and again as if the word alone will break the dreadful spell. I shake her, commanding her to wake up, begging her to open her eyes. She remains pale and silent.

The deities of Olympus come down from their thrones and circle us with curiosity and alarm. My mother shrieks at the sight of the girl in my arms.

"Mother," I bellow, "what have you done?"

"She did this to herself, the fool, opening Persephone's gift to me."

"What gift would Persephone give you?"

The words just out of my mouth, the answer is known to me. The Dread Queen had done my mother the favor of killing the mortal she despises.

I cradle Psyche to me, rocking her and our daughter within her. I feel nothing – no warmth, no breath, no hope. I am too bereft to cry. I can only chant along with the dull thud of my heart:

Too LATE. Too LATE Too LATE.

A mighty voice thunders. "Aphrodite, enough!"

Zeus looms before my mother, his shoulders square, his eyes flashing. She cowers.

"My lord, I had no hand in this."

"You have tormented this poor girl for no reasons other than she is lovely and is loved by your son. She completed your many labors with great bravery and resolve and has proven to be more than worthy for your boy. Eros has plagued me in the past yet even *I* pity him. He must be with his beloved, and she with him. Aphrodite, this stops now."

The lord of Olympus comes to my side. He peers at Psyche then moves his hand over her face. "The sleep of death was upon her, but soon she will be restored."

As he says this she gasps, her eyes spring open, and her body relaxes. She looks at me and all my grief disappears, chased off by her joyous laughter.

"Husband."

"No, my lady, please call me by name. I am Eros."

"Eros." Her voice makes my name sweeter than any music Apollo has played.

###

Since dawn I have been primped and instructed by gentle Demeter and regal Hera in the rites of marriage under Olympus' canopy. Hephaestus has presented me a diadem of finest filigree, alight with pearls. Now I stand at Eros's side, husband in my heart and soon in the eyes of the gods as well.

He is dressed in golden robes, white wings framing his shoulders. He holds my hands within his and his eyes never leave mine: they are blue to the depths, glowing with happiness. Each oath I take is greeted by his wondrous smile, and as he promises to love only me in return, I feel like the sun and stars combined.

Zeus, awesome in his power yet generous with his good nature, officiates. He leavens the solemnities with a wink to Eros, saying, "A wife and child are just what that flighty youth needs to keep him out of future trouble." Then, the ruler of Olympus called for my transformation to begin.

Zeus calls for his cupbearer. A lovely boy brings a draught scented with jasmine and presents it to Eros. He drinks of it then gives it to me.

"Nectar, so your beauty will remain untouched."

I drink it and have never felt so wonderful. It is as if I am abuzz with new wine on a glorious summer day.

The boy brings next a bowl brimming with what appears to be yogurt and honey. Eros tastes some then offers some to me.

"Ambrosia, so you will never age nor die."

As he feeds it to me, my body feels as if it is transformed into streams of sunlight. My senses sparkle and every part of me is vibrant. I am myself and yet so much more. Our daughter leaps in my womb, flush with immortality. Our lives had a beginning; now they will have no end.

We part and I feel a strange itch, as if an insect is crawling down my back under my robes. My shoulders tense and I hear my robes ripping apart. Eros steps back, his face full of wonder. "You are changing."

"What is happening?" I fear perhaps I am being turned into a tree after all.

He finds a mirror and holds it so I can see. "Look here. You have grown wings."

It is as if a giant butterfly has alighted on my back, with wings of gold and black, a blue stripe the color of my lover's eyes hugging the edges. I watch as they float open and closed, amazed to sense the air rippling over and under their silken arcs. I pinch the corner of the left one and flinch. I pull and feel a tug at my spine where they have taken root. It is unbelievably strange, as if my clothing was suddenly part of my skin.

"What does this mean?"

My question is answered by Zeus himself. "I have work for you, dear Psyche."

I bow my head. "How may I serve you, my lord?"

"Your former mortality is a boon to us Olympians. We are a capricious lot and often leave men and women wounded by our actions more than they deserve. You know the human heart because you have one."

The Olympian king brings Eros to my side. "With wings, you are well paired with your husband. When his arrows pierce the hearts of new lovers, you can offer counsel and hope. You can guide them, urge them to be brave as you have been in their pursuit of true love, advise them to trust and not give over to doubt."

He joins our hands. "Eros and Psyche, body and soul. Together they are all love should be."

With this, Zeus consecrates our union and bids us kiss as husband and wife, god and goddess. My eyes stay open as our lips meet. Now that I can see him and all he is, I never want to look away.

The wedding feast is splendid, hosted by Aphrodite herself. While never contrite, she is civil, even pleasant to me as she busies herself with the celebration. Perhaps the gaiety of the party and the delight of becoming a grandmother full of youth and vigor will soften her moods and inspire kind words in the future. Perhaps our truce will become true affection over time.

Hours pass with dancing and music, introductions and blessings until day turns to night. The nuptials complete, we rise together into the air, the wedding guests cheering as we depart. Out of their sight I wobble, my wings an unwieldy nuisance.

"I am barely made immortal, and now I must fly. How can I do this without crashing to the earth?"

His arm circles my waist, his kiss glides across my cheek. "You will find a way. You always do."

We return to our home, our room, our bed. Vases overflow with flowers; the lamps burn low and warm. Soon, our wedding clothes pool at our feet. We step back to take each other in. Two bodies and four wings: we are an unusual pair. We cannot help but laugh as we marvel at who I've become.

He bids me turn my back to him. He runs his fingertip lightly over the wings' edges, and I shiver. He strokes the center of my back and slowly sweeps his hands across their sensitive surfaces, and I bite my lip. He leads me to bed and pulls down the linens; it is odd to see his hands perform the task after so many months of watching the bedclothes moving themselves. We find our place in each other's arms, our unborn child cradled between us, and we kiss, and touch, and connect.

My heart is full.

ABOUT THE AUTHOR

Lisa Peers is the author of *Love and Other B-Sides*, a rock-and-roll love story, and *Eros & Psyche: a Myth of Love Lost and Won*. Born and raised in Richmond, Virginia, she lived in Boston and San Francisco for many years and currently calls Birmingham, Michigan her home.

CPSIA information can be obtained
at www.ICGtesting.com
Printed in the USA
FSHW021956011021
85198FS